To my Dad, for always supporting and
inspiring me. This story wouldn't exist without you.

I.M.

To my mom who was the first to introduce me to art.

O.S.

A TEMPLAR BOOK

First published in the UK in 2023 by Templar Books,
an imprint of Bonnier Books UK
4th Floor, Victoria House,
Bloomsbury Square, London WC1B 4DA
Owned by Bonnier Books
Sveavägen 56, Stockholm, Sweden
www.bonnierbooks.co.uk

1 3 5 7 9 10 8 6 4 2

ISBN 978-1-80078-375-1

Edited by Sophie Hallam
Designed by Anna Ring
Production by Nick Read

Printed in China

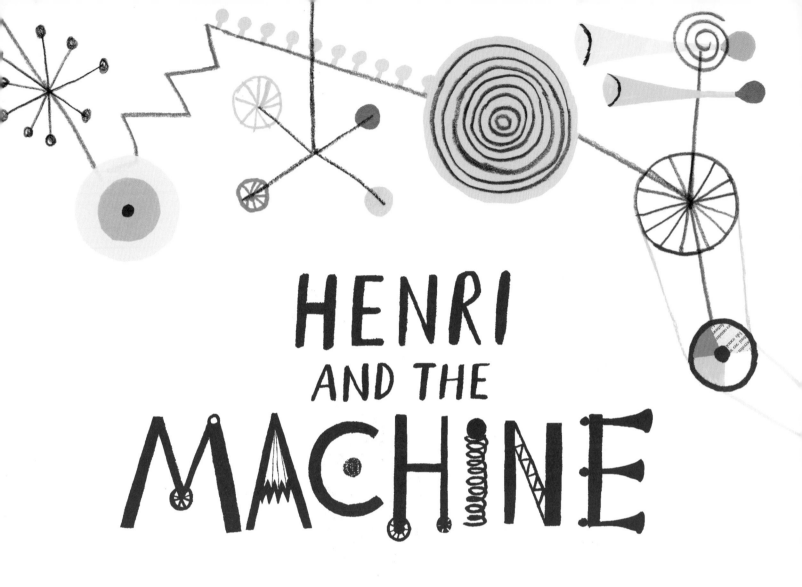

HENRI
AND THE
MACHINE

ISABELLE
MARINOV

OLGA
SHTONDA

templar
books

Everyone seemed happy.
Except for Henri.

He didn't want to go to an art gallery.
He wanted to go to the beach instead.
To collect seashells and to swim
in the ocean.

Henri looked around.
There were lots of paintings on the gallery walls.

A painting of a woman whose eyes were in the wrong place.
Henri knew one thing for sure: both eyes had to be above the nose.

A painting of melting watches. Watches didn't melt.
They broke. They got lost. They stopped. But they did not melt.

A painting of thirty-two soup cans.
Who knew there were that many different kinds of soup?

"Chicken Noodle, Oyster Stew, Pepper Pot, Cream of Celery..."

"No soup in the world deserves a painting!" Henri declared. "But spaghetti with meatballs would. And maybe fish fingers."

But then Henri saw a painting that he liked.

It was all blue; the bluest of blue.

Blue was Henri's favourite colour.

It reminded him of
the ocean,

of blueberries and
summer skies,

blue jays
and butterflies.

The next room was totally empty.

Except for a chair. And a very complicated looking machine.

IS THIS A CHAIR?

¿ES ESTA UNA SILLA?

CZY TO KRZESŁO?

APAKAH INI KURSI?

それは椅子ですか？

IST DAS EIN STUHL?

क्या यह कुर्सी है?

Est-ce une chaise?

هل هذا كرسي؟

ЦЕ СТІЛЕЦЬ?

ONKO SE TUOLI?

这是把椅子吗？

QUESTA È UNA SEDIA?

Ass dëst e Stull?

IS DIT EEN STOEL?

ISTO É UNA CADEIRA?

Είναι μια καρέκλα;

What a strange question, Henri thought. "Of course, it is a chair," he said. "What else could it be?"

"I don't know. In art,
things are never what
they seem. I would not sit
on it," Clara said.

But Henri was tired.
And a tiny bit curious, too.

So he sat down.

BANG!

At that very moment, Henri knew he had set something in motion. Something he could no longer control...

Wheels began turning,
slowly at first...

a tiny marble rolled down a track.

Balloons inflated,
then POPPED!

Drums played and horns honked.

Plates fell to the floor and smashed.

Confetti rained
from a trumpet.

Rainbow-coloured smoke oozed
out of the machine and covered
everything in a technicolour cloud.

And then, the machine fell apart.

The wheels and the marbles,

the drums and the horns...

everything crashed to the ground!

A long, lamenting sound signalled
the end of it all...

The museum guide came running in.
Then he stopped. And looked.

Henri's heart thumped in his chest.
He closed his eyes and wished he could
disappear forever into the blue painting.

"Congratulations," the museum guide cheered.

"Finally, someone sat on that chair! The artist has been waiting for this moment for more than thirty years."

Now Henri was even more confused.
"I thought that art was something
serious?" he asked.

"Art can be many things," the museum guide said.

"It can be playful,

serious,

happy or sad.

It can be something to look at, something to touch or something to sit on.

But all of this doesn't matter.

The only thing that matters is how art makes you feel."

So THAT was the point of art, Henri thought.

"How does The Machine make you feel?"
the museum guide asked.

"It makes me want to giggle,"
Henri said.

PARRRP!